Pokémon™

Kanto Region
I Choose You!

Kanto Region I Choose You!

Adapted by Tracey West

Scholastic Ltd

I Am Ash!

"*A*nd Nidorino begins the battle with a Horn Attack! Oh. But Gengar bounces right back!*" The TV announcer blared the details of the Pokémon fight. The two creatures were battling in a Pokémon Gym. Gengar was a mean-looking Ghost-type Pokémon with glowing red eyes. Nidorino was a tough-looking Poison-type Pokémon with a sharp horn on its forehead.

"*Ah, there it is: the Hypnosis power of Gengar!*"

Gengar clapped its hands together. Pulsing waves flowed from its hands and surrounded Nidorino. Nidorino swayed, captivated by the Hypnosis. It fell to the ground with a thud.

"*This could be the end of Nidorino!*"

A tall man stepped out onto the Gym floor. He held out a red-and-white ball the size of an orange—a Poké Ball. The ball opened and Nidorino disappeared into it with a flash of light.

"Wait! Here comes Nidorino's Trainer. He's recalling Nidorino. Now he can send out another Pokémon to battle Gengar."

Now the Pokémon Trainer held a new Poké Ball. With a great thrust he threw the ball into the ring.

"Which Pokémon will he use now?"

The Pokémon battle raged on. Ash Ketchum watched the fight on his bedroom TV. Someday *he* would be on TV, showing the world that *he* was a great Pokémon Trainer. Someday soon. Now that Ash was ten, he could get his Pokémon license. He could travel around, capturing all the different kinds of Pokémon. He could use his Pokémon in battle against other Pokémon.

Ash grabbed a toy Poké Ball and held it above his head.

"I am Ash!" he cried. "I will journey to gain the wisdom of Pokémon training! I hereby declare to the Pokémon of the world: I will be a Pokémon Master. I will be the greatest—"

"Ash, get to bed!" Ash's mom stood in the doorway. She shook her head. "It's eleven o'clock and you should be asleep."

"But tomorrow I leave Pallet Town and start my Pokémon journey," Ash protested. "I can't sleep!"

Mrs. Ketchum sighed. "If you can't sleep, then you should at least get ready for tomorrow. Here, watch this!" She changed the TV channel. "And don't forget to put on your pajamas!" she called out as she left the room.

A gray-haired man in a lab coat was on the screen. Ash knew him: it was Professor Oak, the world's ultimate authority on Pokémon. His lab was just down the road.

"Good evening, Pallet Town," Professor Oak said. "Tomorrow is the big day for the newest class of Pokémon students!"

The professor pointed to three posters on the wall. Each one showed a Pokémon.

"I'd like to introduce you to Bulbasaur, Charmander, and Squirtle. Each one is available for new trainees. Which one will you choose?"

Ash turned off the TV. He had the same posters on the wall of his room. Every Pokémon Trainer got to pick one of these three Pokémon before they started on their journey. Ash had thought for weeks about which one he would choose, but he still hadn't made a decision.

As Ash put on his pajamas, he looked at the poster of Bulbasaur on his wall. The Grass-type Pokémon was green and had a big flower bulb on its back.

"Bulbasaur is perfect for beginners. I choose you, Bulbasaur!" Ash said aloud.

But then there was Squirtle. The Pokémon looked cute, but Ash knew its Water-type powers could be really strong. "I choose you, Squirtle!" he said.

But what about Charmander? The Fire-type Pokémon had a flaming tail—imagine what he could do with that kind of power!

Ash climbed into bed, but he was too excited to sleep. Bulbasaur . . . Squirtle . . . Charmander . . . Ash tossed and turned. In his dreams, he imagined throwing a Poké Ball and releasing each one into battle. They were all amazing in their own way.

Bulbasaur . . . Squirtle . . . Charmander. How could Ash choose?

CHAPTER 2

A Shocking Start

The Dodrio on a nearby roof screeched and screeched, rousing Ash from his sleep.

He rubbed his eyes and looked out the window. The sun was already high in the sky.

"Oh no!" Ash cried. "I'm late!" He leaped out of bed and ran out of the house.

Squirtle, Bulbasaur, Charmander—any one of them is fine! Just please save one for me! Ash thought as he sped down the road.

Breathless, Ash finally saw Professor Oak's lab up ahead. A long row of steps led up to a hill in the big white building. At the bottom of the hill, a large crowd had formed.

"Gary, Gary, he's our man! If he can't do it, no

one can!" a group of cheerleaders called out.

I've already missed it! Ash thought. He ran through the crowd, accidentally knocking down the cheerleaders.

"Hey, watch where you're going!" said an angry voice.

Ash looked up. He had bumped into Gary, another kid his age and Ash's biggest rival. He was holding a red-and-white Poké Ball.

"S-sorry, Gary," Ash muttered.

"MISTER Gary to you. Show some respect," Gary replied. "Well, Ash, you snooze, you lose. I've got a Pokémon, and you don't."

Ash couldn't believe it. "You got your first Pokémon?"

"That's right, loser, and it's right inside this Poké Ball," Gary said, sneering. "And it's the best one. It helps to have a grandfather in the Pokémon business."

The crowd cheered again. Gary waved and set off on his journey.

Ash's heart sank. Since Professor Oak was Gary's grandfather, he probably *did* get the best Pokémon. *How could I let a bully like Gary beat me?* Ash thought. *I've just got to get one!*

Ash ran up the stairs—right into Professor Oak.

"So you decided to show up after all," the professor said. "Are you sure you are ready?"

"Of course I'm ready!" Ash said.

Professor Oak looked Ash up and down. "You look like you're ready for bed, not for Pokémon training."

Ash cringed. He was still in his pajamas! He was in such a hurry he had forgotten to change his clothes.

Blushing, Ash replied, "I just messed up this morning. I was a little late, but believe me, I'm ready for a Pokémon."

Ash followed Professor Oak up the steps and into the lab. The large room was filled with shiny silver machines. In the center of the room was a silver table with a glass dome on top. Three Poké Balls sat underneath the dome.

Ash began to get excited. He was finally going to get a Pokémon! Professor Oak pushed a button, and the dome opened up.

Ash turned to Professor Oak. "I've thought about it a lot, but I'm not sure which one to choose," Ash said.

Professor Oak opened up the Poké Balls. They were all empty!

"I'm afraid you don't have a choice," he said. "These Pokémon were all taken by Trainers who were on time."

Ash was devastated. "Does this mean I don't get a Pokémon?"

Professor Oak hesitated. "There is one left,

but I'm not sure. There was a problem with this last one."

"I don't care! I'll take it!" Ash pleaded.

The professor pressed a button on the table. A small circular plate in the table's center slid open, and a Poké Ball emerged. The professor handed the ball to Ash. "Here's your Pokémon, Ash."

Ash held the Poké Ball in his hands. A *real* Poké Ball! The ball opened up. Bright flashes of yellow electric light filled the room. When the light stopped, a Pokémon sat on the table in front of him.

"Pikachu," said the Pokémon.

Ash was thrilled. The Pokémon was about a foot tall, bright yellow, with brown stripes on its back. It had pointy ears, red circles on its cheeks, and—best of all—a tail shaped like a lightning bolt.

"That's its name—Pikachu," the professor explained.

"It's so cute!" Ash said. "It's the best one."

The professor smiled nervously. "You'll see."

Ash reached down to pick up the Pokémon. "Hi, Pika—aaaaaah!" A jolt of electricity surged through his body. Pikachu was shocking him!

"Pikachu is a Mouse Pokémon—an Electric type," said the professor. "It's usually shy, but it can sometimes have an electric personality."

"I see what you mean," Ash said, still smarting from Pikachu's charge.

Professor Oak held out his hands. In one hand was a small red electronic device. In the other were six empty Poké Balls.

"This is your Pokédex, which is called Dexter," the professor said. He gave Ash the handheld device. "It is voice activated and can answer all of your questions about Pokémon. It's also your ID and cannot be replaced. So don't lose it."

Professor Oak handed Ash the Poké Balls. "Use these Poké Balls to capture new Pokémon."

"Thanks, Professor Oak," Ash said.

"It's time to begin your journey, Ash."

Ash picked up Pikachu and followed Professor Oak outside. The crowd was still gathered at the bottom of the stairs, banging on instruments and cheering. This time, they were chanting *Ash's* name.

Ash's mom stepped out from the crowd.

"I'm so proud of you!" she said, hugging Ash. She handed Ash a knapsack. "I've packed everything—clothes, clean underwear, your favorite snacks, a clothesline, rubber gloves to do your laundry . . ."

Ash blushed. "Mom, you're embarrassing me in front of all these people!"

"Listen to you mother," the professor said. "Those rubber gloves she packed will come in handy!"

"Why?" asked Ash.

"Rubber blocks electricity," Professor Oak explained.

Ash fished the rubber gloves out of his knapsack. With a Pokémon like Pikachu, he was going to need all the help he could get!

CHAPTER 3

Spearow Attack!

"**P**ikachu, are you going to be like this the whole way?" Ash asked.

"Pi," replied Pikachu stubbornly.

Ash had left Pallet Town and was on his way to Viridian City. Before he left, he changed from pajamas to jeans and his favorite blue-and-white shirt. A baseball cap sat on his messy, dark hair.

He had tied the clothesline around Pikachu's waist and was dragging the Pokémon down the road. But Pikachu didn't want to go anywhere with him.

"Pikachu, why don't you just open your mouth and tell me what's wrong?" Ash asked.

Pikachu opened its mouth wide.

"That's not what I meant. Is your name all you can say?" Ash asked.

"Pika."

"Well then, you should act like other Pokémon and get inside your Poké Ball, just like it says in the Pokédex," Ash said. He flipped open the device.

A mechanical voice spoke, "While being trained, a Pokémon usually stays inside its Poké Ball. However, there are many exceptions. Some Pokémon hate being confined."

"Oh," Ash said. He'd never heard that before.

Ash reached down and untied Pikachu. "This should make things better," he said. "How's that?"

"Pika." Pikachu still didn't look happy.

Ash was about ready to give up when he heard a sound behind him. He turned. It was a wild Pokémon! It was small and had brown and white feathers.

"A Pidgey!" Ash cried.

"Pidgey is a Flying-type Pokémon. It is easy to capture. A perfect target for the beginning Trainer," said Dexter the Pokédex.

Ash was thrilled. "Go get it, Pikachu!" he called out.

"Chu." Pikachu turned its head away.

"Aren't you ever going to listen to me?" Ash asked

"Chu."

Ash was starting to get mad. Of all the Pokémon in the world, he had to get one that didn't like him. "Why won't you help?" he pleaded.

Pikachu hopped onto a tree branch and began to chirp like a Pidgey. *"Pika pika pika!"* Then Pikachu started laughing.

Ash knew it was mocking him. "I get the message. I don't need your help. I can get that thing all by myself."

Ash pulled a Poké Ball from his knapsack. He faced Pidgey. "Enjoy your last moments of freedom, Pidgey. You're mine!"

Ash threw the ball at Pidgey. "Poké Ball, go!" he yelled.

The ball flew through the air. It hit Pidgey, then opened up. A flash of red light burst from the ball, and Pidgey disappeared. The ball closed.

Ash cheered. "I did it!"

Suddenly, the ball began to shake. It opened again. Pidgey escaped in a blaze of white light!

Ash couldn't believe it.

"Pika-ha-ha-ha!" Pikachu was laughing on its tree branch.

The Pokédex spoke. "To capture a Pokémon, you usually have your own Pokémon battle with the other Pokémon."

"But it's not fair!" Ash said. "My own Pokémon won't even help me."

Ash wasn't about to give up. He picked up a rock and looked around. Not far away was a flock of Pidgey just waiting to be captured.

Ash threw the rock. It landed on the ground, scattering the Pidgey.

Quickly, Ash, spotted another flying Pokémon. He picked up another rock. "I'll get you this time!" Ash yelled.

He did it! The rock tapped the Pokémon right on the head.

The Pokémon turned around and looked at Ash angrily. This was no Pidgey, Ash knew. This one had a long, curved beak. It looked mean.

"Wonder what that is?" Ash asked nervously.

"Unlike Pidgey, Spearow has a terrible temper," Dexter said. "It is very wild and will sometimes attack other Pokémon."

Ash didn't have time to react to the news, because Spearow was in the air—and it was flying right at Pikachu!

"Hey, leave Pikachu alone! It didn't throw the rock!" Ash yelled.

"Wild Pokémon tend to be jealous of human-trained Pokémon," explained the Pokédex.

Spearow swooped down on Pikachu. Pikachu lost its footing and slipped off the tree branch. Just in time, it grabbed the branch with its hands.

"Pikachuuu!" screamed Pikachu in fear.

Spearow flew directly at Pikachu. Ash watched helplessly from the ground.

Suddenly, Pikachu let off an electric shock. Bright light crackled in the air. The shock sent Spearow flying backward.

"You got it!" Ash cried. He reached out and pulled Pikachu toward him.

"*Speeeeeeearow!*" A strange cry filled the air. In the distance, Ash saw a whole flock of Spearow. The flying Pokémon were speeding toward them!

Ash and Pikachu ran down the road. Pikachu scurried ahead. The Spearow were closing in.

Ash watched in horror as three Spearow swooped down and grabbed at Pikachu with their sharp beaks. Ash charged ahead and picked up Pikachu. The Spearow seemed to be everywhere. They pecked at Ash's head and arms.

Ash ran and ran with Pikachu on his back. His heart was pounding. How could they escape?

Ash looked ahead. His heart sank. The road ended in a steep cliff.

They were trapped!

Ask skidded to a stop at the cliff's edge. He looked down. Below him was a roaring waterfall that led into a swift river.

He looked behind him. The sky was filled with screeching Spearow.

Ash took a deep breath. He had no choice.

"Here we go, Pikachu!" he yelled.

Ash closed his eyes, held Pikachu tightly, and plunged into the raging waterfall!

CHAPTER 4

Thundershock!

Ash's stomach plunged as the waterfall carried him and Pikachu down into the water. When they hit the surface of the river, the force of the waterfall sent them spiraling into the water's depths. *I've got to swim to the surface!* Ash thought frantically.

Ash kicked with all his might. He pushed through the water with one hand and held Pikachu with the other. He thought his lungs would burst. Suddenly, he felt someone pull on his shirt collar. He was being yanked out of the water!

Ash slammed onto the shore, gasping for air.

He opened his eyes. A red-haired girl with a fishing pole was staring at them.

"I thought I caught a fish," the girl said. "But it looks like I caught a kid—*and* a Pokémon. I'm Misty. Are you okay?"

Ash spit water out of his mouth. "I . . . I think so," he said.

Misty scowled. "Not you! Your Pokémon. Look what you've done to it. Is it breathing?"

Ash glanced at Pikachu. Its eyes were closed, and it wasn't moving.

"I'm not sure," Ash said weakly.

"Well, don't just sit there! It needs a doctor right away," Misty said. "There's a medical center for Pokémon nearby."

Flap flap flap flap flap.

Panicked, Ash's eyes scanned the sky. The Spearow had found them, and they were bearing down fast!

"They're coming back!" Ash yelled. There was a red bike propped up nearby. Ash put Pikachu in the bike basket and hopped onto the seat.

"Hey, that's my bike!" Misty cried.

Ash began pedaling down the road. "I need to borrow it! But I'll bring it back someday!" he called back.

Ash pedaled furiously. Black storm clouds gathered low in the sky overhead. Thunder rumbled in the distance. But it couldn't mask the sound of the Spearow. They were getting closer.

"Speeeeearow!"

"Hang on, Pikachu! We're almost there!" Ash tried to reassure the Pokémon, but he was afraid. The Spearow were all around.

Suddenly, Ash felt the ground give way beneath him. They were flying over a ridge! The wheels hit the road below, but Ash lost control. He watched as Pikachu flew out of the basket and landed a few feet away.

A bolt of lightning flashed in the sky. Raindrops pelted Ash's body. The sky was filled with attacking Spearow. They swooped and lunged at him and Pikachu, getting closer each time.

Pikachu. I have to protect it. That was Ash's only thought.

Ash took a Poké Ball out of his knapsack and ran to Pikachu's motionless body.

"Pikachu, you've got to get inside the ball. Maybe I can save you. Please trust me," Ash pleaded.

"*Chuuu,*" Pikachu said. Ash saw that Pikachu was too weak to move.

It's up to me now, Ash realized. He stood up and faced the attacking Spearow.

"Spearow, do you know who I am?" Ash yelled. "I'm Ash from Pallet Town. I can't be defeated by the likes of you. I'm going to capture you all! Do you hear me?"

Behind him, Pikachu opened its eyes.

"Pikachu, get inside the Poké Ball," Ash said softly.

An earsplitting thunderclap roared. A bright flash of lightning pierced the sky. The Spearow paused in midair, then aimed their beaks at Ash.

Ash stood firm. He wasn't running away this time. "Come and get me!" Ash yelled.

The Spearow charged Ash!

From the corner of his eye, Ash saw something fly past him.

Pikachu!

Pikachu was jumping between Ash and the Spearow!

"Nooooooo!"

A clap of thunder drowned out Ash's cry. Time seemed to stand still as a lightning bolt illuminated the air. Pikachu jumped right into the lightning bolt. Pikachu's body glowed with electricity as it bonded with the lightning. The impact created a huge explosion.

A Thundershock!

CHAPTER 5

Pokémon Emergency!

A blazing ball of white light lit up the sky.
Ash was thrown backward by the blast.
He was stunned. The blast was bigger than
lightning. Bigger than fireworks. He couldn't
believe it!

Ash looked beside him. Pikachu was
lying next to him. Above them, the clouds
disappeared. The sun shone in the blue sky.
There were no Spearow to be seen.

Pikachu had risked its life to save Ash!

"We beat them," Ash said, exhausted.

"Chuuu," Pikachu replied. Pikachu was alive,
but it looked hurt. Really hurt.

Ash knew his troubles weren't over yet. He

had to get Pikachu to the Pokémon Center—before it was too late!

Ash looked at Misty's bike. The metal was charred and black from the explosion. They'd have to go on foot.

Down the road, Ash could see the buildings of Viridian City. He could make it, but he'd have to hurry.

Ash ran with Pikachu in his arms. The trees on the roadside grew farther and farther apart. A paved road lay ahead of them. They had made it!

As they got closer, the sound of a siren wailed in the air.

"Attention, citizens of Viridian City!" blared a voice from a loudspeaker. *"We have reports of possible Pokémon thieves in our area. Be on the lookout for suspicious-looking strangers."*

Pokémon thieves? That sounds dangerous, Ash thought. But he didn't have time to stop. Pikachu needed help—fast. Ash ran down the streets of Viridian City. A large dome-shaped building with a red "P" on the front loomed before him.

"The Pokémon Center!" Ash cried. "It's gigantic." He charged through the front doors. "Please help my Pikachu," Ash told the nurse behind the desk.

The nurse took one look at Pikachu and began typing into the computer. "I need a stretcher for a small Electric-type Pokémon, stat!" she ordered.

The emergency room door opened, and two chubby pink Pokémon wearing nurse's caps emerged, wheeling a stretcher. The nurse took Pikachu from Ash's arms and put it on the stretcher. Poor Pikachu looked so hurt! Ash could barely watch as the Pokémon nurses wheeled it away.

The human nurse put a hand on Ash's shoulder. Her red hair was tied up in two ponytails, and

Ash thought she had a sweet face. "It'll be okay. We'll take good care of it. Chansey Pokémon are very good nurses. I'm Joy. Who are you?"

"I'm Ash," he said, "Pikachu's Trainer."

Joy's expression clouded. "I hope you're more responsible in the future, Ash. You should never let a Pokémon battle when it's in this condition."

Ash stared at the floor. He knew Joy was right.

Joy stepped behind two sliding metal doors. "Ash, you'll have to go to the waiting room," she said.

"But I want to—" Ash started, but the doors closed in front of him.

Ash stepped into the waiting room. Telephones with video screens lined one wall. One of them was ringing.

Ash found the phone that was ringing and flipped on the screen. Professor Oak's face appeared before him.

"Ah, Ash. I was hoping you would have reached Viridian City by now," the professor said. "All of the other Trainers from Pallet Town are there. I'm pleasantly surprised you got there so soon."

Ash blushed.

The professor continued, "In fact, when my grandson Gary said you wouldn't have any new Pokémon by the time you got there, I bet him a million dollars he'd be wrong!"

Ash turned bright red. "Well, money isn't everything, right?"

"Oh, why do I even bother?" Professor Oak sighed. A bell rang. "Ash, I've got to go. My pizza's here." The screen went blank.

What a rotten day! Ash thought. *My Pokémon is hurt. Gary Oak beat me here. Professor Oak thinks I'm a loser. What else could go wrong?*

"I knew I'd find you here!"

Ash whirled around at the sound of the angry

voice. It was Misty! She carried the burned bike on her shoulder.

"You are going to pay for what you did to my bike!" Misty fumed.

Ash collapsed in a chair. It was all just too much.

"I'll make up for it when I can," Ash said. "But right now, I've got to take care of my Pikachu."

Misty's face softened. "Is it all right?"

The emergency room doors swung open. Joy and the two Chansey Pokémon wheeled Pikachu in on a stretcher. Pikachu had a metal strip wrapped around its head. A lightbulb was attached to the strip. Wires connected the headgear to a metal pole on wheels.

Ash rushed to Pikachu's side. "Are you all right?" he asked.

Pikachu's eyes were closed. It didn't answer.

"The procedure went well. Your Pikachu should be fine," Joy said.

Ash breathed a sigh of relief. "Thank you so much!" Maybe things were finally looking up.

Ash jumped as a loud siren blasted through the Pokémon Center.

"Attention, Viridian City!" blared a voice from the loudspeaker. *"Our sensors have detected an aircraft belonging to a gang of Pokémon thieves."*

"What now?" Ash asked.

A loud crash answered his question. Ash looked up.

Two Poké Balls crashed through the glass roof of the Pokémon Center.

Clouds of thick green smoke began to fill the waiting room. Ash choked. The foul-smelling smoke smelled like poison.

They were under attack!

CHAPTER 6

Team Rocket Blasts Off

Two Pokémon emerged from the green smoke. One looked like a purple cloud and floated in the air. The smoke was coming from its body.

"Koffing!" it said in a deep voice.

The other Pokémon slithered across the floor.

"Ekans!" hissed the snakelike Pokémon.

The smoke cleared, and a teenage boy and girl stepped into the waiting room. They wore black boots and white uniforms with the letter "R" on their shirts. Between them was a cream-colored Pokémon with big whiskers.

"Who are they?" Ash asked, coughing.

"Allow us to introduce ourselves," said the boy.

"To protect the world from devastation," said the girl.

"To unite all peoples within our nation," said the boy.

"To denounce the evils of truth and love," said the girl.

"To extend our reach to the stars above," said the boy.

"Jessie!" said the girl.

"James!" said the boy.

"Team Rocket—blast off at the speed of light!" said Jessie.

"Surrender now or prepare to fight!" said James.

"*Meowth!* That's right," chimed in the whiskered Pokémon.

Ash looked at Joy and Misty. "What are they talking about?" he asked.

"We're here for the Pokémon!" James demanded.

Ash ran to Pikachu's side. "You're NOT getting Pikachu!" he cried.

Jesse sneered. "We're not interested in your precious electric rat."

"We seek only rare and valuable Pokémon," James said. "Koffing, attack!"

More green smoke poured from Koffing's body as the Pokémon charged toward them. Ash pushed Pikachu's stretcher and sped down the nearest hallway, with Misty and Joy at his heels.

"In here!" Joy cried, leading them through a door.

Ash leaned against the door, breathless. Koffing and Ekans had lost their trail. They were safe—for now.

Suddenly, the lights went out.

"They must have cut the power!" Joy cried. "But that's okay. We've got our own 'Pika Power' source."

Ash watched as small bolts of electricity crackled in the center of the room. The lights came back on. A group of Pikachu were running in place on a round platform in the center of the room. They were creating the electricity.

With the light on, Ash saw that the room was filled with Poké Balls. He guessed that they probably contained sick or injured Pokémon.

Joy ran to a computer and turned it on. "This is the Viridian City Pokémon Center. We have an emergency situation. Transporting Poké Balls."

"This is the Pewter City Pokémon Center," a voice replied. "Ready to receive Poké Balls."

At Joy's command, a mechanical arm began lifting up the balls one by one and putting them in a conveyor. The belt led to a transportation device. As each ball hit the transport center, it was struck by a beam of light—then disappeared.

Suddenly, Koffing and Ekans crashed through the door, sending the Poké Balls flying. Team Rocket and Meowth were right behind them.

Misty looked angry. She picked up a Poké Ball. "This is war!"

Ash understood. He picked up a ball and threw it at Ekans. "Poké Ball, go!" he yelled.

The ball opened, and Pidgey appeared in a blast of light.

"Ekans!" hissed the snake Pokémon.

Terrified, Pidgey flew back into the ball.

"I'll take care of these clowns," Misty told Ash. "You take Pikachu and get out of here."

"Right!" Ash said. He wasn't going to let Pikachu get hurt again. Not this time.

Ash pushed Pikachu down the hallway. Behind him, he could hear Team Rocket laughing. Whatever Misty was doing wasn't working.

The smell of smoke burned his nostrils. Ash looked behind him.

It was Koffing and Ekans. They were closing in fast.

There was no escape!

CHAPTER 7

Pika Power

Ash wheeled Pikachu into the waiting room and headed for the door.

Crash! He smashed into Misty's busted bike.

With the impact, Pikachu opened its eyes and sat up.

"Pika pika," it said in a daze.

Koffing and Ekans eyed Pikachu hungrily. Ash knew Pikachu was still too weak to take on these two creeps.

Team Rocket ran in. Misty was behind them.

"I couldn't stop them!" she cried.

Jessie laughed. "It's all over now!"

A low rumbling sound filled the room.

Pikachu were pouring into the room from every doorway. Ash had never seen so many!

The Pikachu jumped on Ash's Pikachu's stretcher.

"Pika pika chu chu! Pika pika chu chu!" they cried.

Ash watched in amazement as all the Pikachu created an electric charge. The air around them glowed with yellow light. The Pikachu chanting got louder and louder. Then they hurled the charge—right at Team Rocket!

Meowth leaped out of the way as the charge electrified Jessie, James, Koffing, and Ekans. They all fell to the floor in a heap. *"Pikachu!"* cheered the group of Pikachu.

Ash rushed to his Pikachu's side. Pikachu was standing up.

Ash turned at the sound of Meowth's voice.

"Do I have to do everything?" Meowth shouted. "That mouse is cat food! You're mine, Pikachu!" Meowth lunged at them.

"Pika . . . pika pika," Pikachu said.

Ash knew Pikachu was trying to tell him something. "Pika pika?" Ash asked.

"Pika," Pikachu said again.

"Pika power?" Ash asked. He finally understood. "You want . . . more power!"

Ash jumped on Misty's bike and began to pedal. The bike was too busted up to move, but the bike's headlight was still working. It shone brighter and brighter the more Ash pedaled.

"What's this?" Meowth asked.

"Let's just say that Pikachu and I are going to generate a little excitement!" Ash replied.

Pikachu jumped onto the shining light. Ash could see the electric charge coursing through Pikachu's body.

"Oh no," Jessie said.

"You can say that again," said James.

Ash closed his eyes and braced himself. His hair was standing on end from all the electricity Pikachu was creating.

"Pika . . . Chu!" Pikachu cried as it released a huge electric charge. A loud explosion rocked the Pokémon Center. Orange flames shot into the sky. Ash was blinded by the bright like. Slowly, he opened his eyes and looked around.

The Pokémon Center was in ruins. But Pikachu was beside Ash, smiling. Pikachu was all right!

Nurse Joy stepped over the rubble. "It's a good thing I got all those Pokémon transported safely to Pewter City," she said.

The Ash saw Misty. She was covered in dust, but she was all right, too. "I'm not sure what you did," she said. "But it looks like you got rid of Team Rocket."

Ash looked around. There was no sign of Jessie, James, or Meowth anywhere.

"I'll bet they'll think twice before messing with us again," Ash said. But deep down, he wasn't so sure.

High over Viridian City, Team Rocket made its escape in their hot-air balloon. Their once-sparkling uniforms were charred and torn.

Jessie scowled at Meowth. "A cat losing to a mouse! I can't believe it."

"That Pikachu is no ordinary Pikachu!" Meowth protested.

James looked thoughtful. "It's certainly very *rare*. And our mission *is* to capture all rare Pokémon for our boss. It would be a perfect prize."

"Let's catch it!" Jessie said.

"*Meowth!* You're ours, Pikachu," Meowth purred as the balloon floated away.

CHAPTER 8

Vermilion City

"**W**e made it! It's Vermilion City!"
Ash couldn't believe how far he had
come since he left Pallet Town to begin his
Pokémon training. At first, he had a Pikachu
that didn't like him and no friends to count on.

He and Pikachu had been through a lot
together, and now they were friends. After Ash
tried so hard to protect Pikachu in Viridian City,
Pikachu forgave Ash for being so demanding
at first. And defeating Team Rocket together
had felt really good. Now Ash could understand
Pikachu when it spoke—although Pikachu *still*
wouldn't get inside a Poké Ball.

Misty had decided to come along with Ash

to complete her Pokémon training, too. And on the way to Vermillion City, they had made a new friend, Brock. Brock was older than Ash and Misty—a Gym Leader who had put his journey on hold to take care of his little brothers and sisters. Now Brock was back on the road. Ash felt like he could do anything with his team of friends behind him.

"We made it! It's good to be in a new city," Brock said as the friends gazed at the city sprawled out before them.

"I'm going to hit the Vermilion City Gym—right now!" Ash said.

Brock grabbed Ash by the collar. "No, you're not!"

"But I have to!" Ash said. "Every Trainer has to battle its Pokémon against the Gym Leader's Pokémon in each new city. If I win a battle, I'll earn a badge. And I don't have many yet! Without badges, I'll never be able to control higher-level Pokémon."

"No kidding," Misty said. "But look at Pikachu!"

Pikachu was lying weakly on the ground. Its stomach was growling.

"We haven't eaten anything decent for three days now," Brock reminded him.

Ash knew Brock was right. "All right. Let's head for the Pokémon Center first," he said reluctantly.

The dome-shaped Pokémon Center looked a lot like the one in Viridian City. Pikachu was quickly swept away to the recovery room. Ash, Misty, and Brock looked around. The hospital ward was filled with injured Pokémon and concerned Trainers.

A nurse, whose name was also Joy, greeted them. "They all lost to Lieutenant Surge, the Vermilion Gym Leader," she explained.

"Whoa! He must be a great Trainer," Ash said. A bell rang softly in the ward.

"That sound means your Pokémon has recovered," Nurse Joy said, leading them back into the lobby. Pikachu was sitting on a table, happily eating apples.

"I'm glad you're feeling so much better, Pikachu," Ash said. "We're going to win big at that Gym today!"

"Pi!" said Pikachu. It looked ready to fight.

The front doors slid open again. Another Trainer burst in, wheeling a Pidgey on a stretcher. The Pidgey looked badly hurt.

"I guess they must've come from the Gym," Misty said.

Pikachu looked alarmed. *"Pikachu! Pikachu!"* the Pokémon waved its arms excitedly. *"Pika. Pikachu!"*

"What?" Ash asked. Usually he could understand what Pikachu was trying to say. "You mean you don't want to end up like that Pidgey there?"

"Pika! Pika!" Pikachu nodded yes.

"I guess you're right," Ash said.

Pikachu breathed a sigh of relief.

"You won't end up that way," Ash continued. "Because you'll win!"

"Chu . . . Chu!" Pikachu shook its head stubbornly.

"Don't be a scaredy-cat," Ash said. He turned to Misty and Brock. "Next stop, Vermilion Gym!"

CHAPTER 9

Pikachu vs. Raichu

"**S**o this is the Vermilion City Gym," Ash said. The huge building towered above them. Lightning bolts decorated the doors.

"It's not too late to back out," Misty said.

"Why should I back out when I'm going to win?" Ash asked. "Just stick around and watch me!"

"I'll stick around to watch your face when you get creamed!" Misty teased. "You haven't had a lot of battle experience, and this Surge guy sounds like he's really tough."

Brock was impatient. "Are we ever going to go inside?"

At Brock's words, the large Gym doors swung open.

A tall, blond-haired man stood inside. Huge muscles bulged beneath his uniform.

"Which one of you is the challenger?" Surge grunted.

Ash stepped forward. "I am. Ash Ketchum."

Surge patted Ash's head. "How cute. Don't think I'll go easy on you, baby."

"Hey, I'm no baby!" Ash protested.

"I call everyone who loses to me 'baby,'" Surge said.

Pikachu clung to Ash's leg nervously.

Surge laughed. "A Pikachu? So the baby has a baby Pokémon!"

"Quit it!" Ash said. "Why are you making fun of my Pokémon?"

The Gym Leader pulled a Poké Ball from his pocket. "I'll show you why. Go, Poké Ball!"

Surge threw the ball. There was a flash of light, and a Pokémon appeared.

Ash gasped. The Pokémon looked kind of like Pikachu, only bigger, and it was a yellow-orange color. Its long, thin tail ended in a lightning bolt. "It's a Raichu!" Ash exclaimed.

The Pokédex spoke, "Raichu is the evolved form of Pikachu. A Pikachu can become a Raichu with the use of a Thunder Stone. Raichu can shock with more than one hundred thousand volts."

Pikachu growled at the Raichu.

"You should have made your Pokémon evolve as soon as you got it," Surge said. "Like I did. Electric-type Pokémon are only useful once they've learned all the electric attacks. Are you sure you don't want to quit?"

Ash looked at Pikachu. Angry sparks shot from its face. He knew it wanted to battle.

Ash faced Surge. "Let's do it!"

Still laughing, Surge led Ash and his team to the Gym floor. Surge and Raichu stood on one side of the Gym, and Ash and Pikachu stood on the other side.

"In this battle, only one Pokémon may be used," blared the Gym announcer. *"Let the battle begin!"*

A bell rang. Raichu and Pikachu ran into the center of the Gym and faced each other.

"Pikachu, Thundershock!" Ash commanded.

Pikachu hurled a large blast of electricity at Raichu.

"Pika . . . chu!"

The blast hit Raichu. To Ash's amazement, the Pokémon absorbed the shock. It wasn't fazed at all.

"Raichu! Show them a *real* Thundershock!" Surge ordered.

A glowing yellow light surrounded Raichu. The Pokémon fired an electric blast directly at Pikachu.

"*Rai . . . chu!*"

The huge blast hit Pikachu at full force. Pikachu went flying across the Gym.

Pikachu slowly rose to its feet. It was weak. But it wasn't going to give in.

"Raichu, Mega Punch!" Surge cried.

Before Pikachu could react, Raichu aimed a powerful punch at Pikachu's body. Pikachu crashed to the floor.

This time, Pikachu didn't get up.

"The battle is over!" Surge cried.

Ash rushed Pikachu to the Pokémon Center. Soon Pikachu lay in a hospital bed, its head and body covered in bandages.

"Pikachu's spirit got hurt pretty badly," Brock said. "It was overpowered by Raichu."

"Brock's right," Misty said.

"We'll win next time," Ash said.

"There *is* one way you might win."

Nurse Joy stepped into the room. She held a small red box.

"You could use this," she said. She handed the box to Ash.

Ash opened the lid. Inside was a shining crystal.

"Wow, it's a Thunder Stone!" Brock cried. "You could use it to evolve Pikachu into a Raichu."

"Then Pikachu might become strong enough to win," Ash realized.

"If you make Pikachu evolve," Joy warned, "you can't change it back."

Ash didn't know what to do. "If Pikachu becomes Raichu, I could win that badge," he said. "But if I made it evolve just so it could fight, I would be just like Surge. He doesn't care about his Pokémon. He only cares about winning."

Ash turned to Pikachu. "What do *you* want to do, Pikachu? This is your choice, not mine."

Pikachu stood up. It looked hard at Ash.

Then it knocked the Thunder Stone out of Ash's hands with its tail.

"Pika! Pika!" Pikachu said.

Ash understood. "Pikachu, together you and I will beat Lieutenant Surge and his Raichu."

"You're both crazy!" Misty said.

Brock looked thoughtful. "Hey, Ash. Surge said that he had made his Raichu evolve as soon as he got it, didn't he?"

Ash nodded.

"Then maybe there is a way to win," Brock said.

"Pika pika pika!"

Outside the Pokémon Center, Team Rocket peered at the scene through a window.

"Meowth, what is Pikachu saying?" Jessie asked.

Meowth was sniffling. "Pikachu is so brave! It says it won't change. It's going to fight in the name of all Pikachu!"

James brushed a tear from his eye. "Oh dear. That's magnificent."

"If Pikachu wins this battle," Jessie said, "we will simply *have* to capture it!"

CHAPTER 10

Electric Shock Showdown!

The bright Gym lights glared in Ash's face. Across the Gym, Surge and Raichu faced them.

"You didn't even make your Pikachu evolve. You haven't learned anything yet," Surge jeered.

Ash stood firm. Surge wasn't going to beat him. This time was different.

This time they had a plan.

"The challenger, Ash, using a Pikachu!" blared the announcer. *"The Gym Leader, Lieutenant Surge, using a Raichu! The Pokémon will battle one-on-one. Let the battle begin!"*

"Use the strategy we planned, Pikachu!" Ash called out.

"A strategy! So they've been planning a new way to lose," Surge mocked. He turned to his Pokémon. "Go, Raichu!"

Raichu lashed out at Pikachu with the lightning bolt at the end of its tail. The blow sent Pikachu sprawling across the floor. Every time Pikachu tried to get up, Raichu's tail lashed out again.

"Now a Body Slam, Raichu!" Surge yelled.

Pikachu was dazed, lying facedown on the floor. *Slam!* Raichu threw its body on top of Pikachu.

"Hang in there, Pikachu!" Misty called.

Slam! Raichu pummeled Pikachu again.

"Roll to the side and break away!" Brock called out.

Raichu threw itself at Pikachu again. This time, Pikachu reacted. It quickly rolled out of the way. *Slam!* Raichu thudded against the floor.

"Do it, Pikachu! Agility, now!" Ash coached.

Pikachu sped toward Raichu. Raichu threw its body at Pikachu.

Slam! Pikachu ran out of the way.

Slam! Raichu missed again.

Slam! Raichu pounded against the floor.

"It's working!" Misty shouted.

"Right," Brock explained. "Raichu evolved too fast. It never learned the speed attacks it could only learn at the Pikachu stage."

Pikachu was running circles around Raichu. The larger Pokémon spun around, trying to catch it. Ash could see Raichu was growing dizzy.

Thud! Raichu fell down in a daze.

Ash was thrilled. "Your Raichu is way too slow, Surge. That's its weakness."

"Raichu, give it a Thunderbolt! Shut it down!" Surge ordered angrily.

Raichu rose to its feet. It raised its arms and let out a piercing cry.

"Rai . . . chuuuuuuu!"

A huge electric charge exploded from Raichu's body. Ash felt the Gym floor rumble.

The Gym rocked in a blaze of white light. Glass windows shattered. Ash was knocked off his feet.

"This match is over!" Surge bragged.

Ash opened his eyes. The Gym was destroyed. But in the center of the floor was Pikachu. It wasn't hurt!

Pikachu's tail was sticking straight up out of the floor.

"Pikachu used its tail as a ground and dodged the electric shock," Brock said.

"Pika!" Pikachu looked angry.

"Raichu! Give it another Thunderbolt!" Surge commanded.

Raichu closed its eyes. It focused with all its might and tried to throw out a Thunderbolt.

Nothing happened.

Surge looked panicked. "Do something, Raichu!"

"It's over," Brock said. "Raichu ran out of electricity."

Ash turned to Pikachu. "Quick Attack!"

Pikachu charged at Raichu and slammed against its body. Weakened, Raichu toppled to the floor.

"Raichu! Now!" Surge yelled.

Pikachu charged into Raichu again. Pikachu's tail began to glow with electric light. Pikachu swung around and shocked Raichu with a powerful blast of electricity. The charge coursed through Raichu's body.

Raichu shook with the charge. Then it lay still. It was knocked out!

"*Now* this match is over!" Ash said.

Surge crossed the Gym and held out his hand. "Congratulations!" He passed something into Ash's palm. "As proof of your victory."

Ash opened his hand. A yellow-orange stone glittered against a gold sunburst. "I can't believe it! It's a Thunder Badge!"

"You and your Pikachu really fought well together," Surge admitted. "Ash, you're no baby."

"Rai!" Raichu was back on its feet. It smiled at Pikachu.

"Pika!" Pikachu replied.

Ash hugged Pikachu. "Thanks, Pikachu. This was your victory."

"Pika!" Pikachu jolted Ash with a friendly blast of electricity.

Misty laughed. "Those two really are quite a team!"

*   *   *

Outside the Gym, Team Rocket celebrated.

"That Pikachu is really special," said James.

Jessie nodded. "Yes, and that's why it's worth stealing!"

"You're right," James said. "We've wasted enough time. Soon Ash will find out just how deliciously evil Team Rocket really is!"

Meowth grinned. *"Meowth!* You can say that again."

CHAPTER 11

Pikachu Goes Wild

"What a great place this is for a rest," Misty said.

Brock nodded. "Yeah, it's nice to kick back and relax a little."

Ash took a deep breath of clean air. The tall trees of the forest towered above their campsite.

"This is a great place," Ash agreed. "We definitely need a vacation after all we've been through."

"Pika!"

Pikachu was perched on a tree branch, eating an apple. It made Ash feel good to see Pikachu look so happy.

"Pika?" With a start, Pikachu scrambled down the tree trunk and ran out of the campsite.

"Hey! Where are you going, Pikachu?" Ash called. He took off running after his Pokémon. Misty and Brock were right behind him.

Pikachu stopped at the edge of a clearing in the forest. Ash crashed to a stop behind it.

"It's amazing!" Misty whispered, looking into the clearing.

A herd of Pikachu were gathered a few yards away. Ash had never seen so many in one place. The Pikachu were eating apples and playing games.

"Those must be wild Pikachu," Brock guessed.

"Pika!" Pikachu said excitedly. It ran out into the clearing. *"Pika pi!"*

The wild Pikachu froze and stared at Pikachu.

"Pikachu!" Pikachu waved hello.

"Chuuu!" the herd scattered, running to the other side of the clearing.

They're not sure if they should accept Pikachu, Ash realized.

Pikachu looked sad. Its ears drooped. A tiny Pikachu slowly emerged from the herd. It carefully approached Pikachu. The tiny Pikachu lifted up its head and sniffed Piakchu's nose.

"Pi!" squeaked the tiny Pikachu. It turned around and offered Pikachu its tail.

Pikachu smiled. It tapped its tail against the tiny Piakchu's tail.

The wild Pikachu looked at one another. Then they gave a happy cry and ran toward Pikachu. They surrounded Pikachu and began chattering away.

"It looks like they've accepted Pikachu as part of their group," Brock said.

"All right!" Ash said. This was really exciting. He ran out into the clearing.

"Hey! I want to be a part of your group, too!" Ash yelled, waving his arms.

Pikachu saw Ash and waved back. But the wild Pikachu screamed and ran out of the clearing.

"Don't run away!" Ash called out.

"Quit it, Ash," Misty said.

Ash spun around. "What do you mean?"

"Don't you get it, Ash?" Brock asked. "Those Pikachu are scared of you. They're not used to humans."

"Pi," Pikachu said sadly. It stared into the empty clearing.

Ash sighed. "I'm sorry, Pikachu."

Ash kicked at the dirt and headed back toward the campsite.

I always ruin everything, Ash thought. *Sometimes I think Pikachu would be better off without me.*

*   *   *

69

On a nearby tree branch, Team Rocket watched the herd of Pikachu through binoculars.

"If we turn all these Pikachu over to the boss . . ." Jessie began.

"We'll be promoted for sure," James finished.

"Piles of Pikachu everywhere! *Meowth!*" added their Pokémon.

James grinned.

"To the balloon!" he said. "We've got work to do."

CHAPTER 12

Trapped by
Team Rocket

"**P**ika pika pikachu!"

The sound of the wild Pikachu singing floated in the night air. A bright moon hung in the sky. Brock and Misty slept peacefully next to the campfire.

Ash couldn't sleep. He poked at the fire with a stick. Pikachu had made friends with the herd of wild Pikachu and was off playing with them in the forest. He seemed so happy with them! Staring into the fire, Ash could almost see Pikachu's face smiling at him.

"I think it's the best thing in the world for

Pikachu to be with its own kind," Brock had told him. Ash knew he was probably right. But now that they were such good friends, the thought of life without Pikachu hurt.

A small breeze kicked up, blowing out the campfire. Ash watched sadly as the image of Pikachu died with the flames.

"Piiiiiiiiiiiiiiiiiiiiiiiiiiiii!"

A terrified cry pierced the night air. Ash tensed. It was the wild Pikachu!

Misty and Brock snapped awake.

"Let's go!" Ash cried. Brock and Misty followed Ash through the forest and into the clearing.

Ash gasped. The wild Pikachu were piled in a heap in the center of the clearing. A thick net surrounded them.

Ash spotted his Pikachu in the net. Pikachu was trapped, too!

"Pikachu!" Ash cried out.

Suddenly, white light filled the clearing. Ash shielded his eyes.

"What's going on?" Ash asked.

The sound of evil laughter echoed through the forest. Then Ash heard Team Rocket's battle cry.

". . . Team Rocket—blast off at the speed of light! Surrender now, or prepare to fight!"

It can't be, Ash thought, but Jessie, James, and Meowth jumped down from the nearby tree and into the clearing.

"Stand back while we swipe these Pikachu!" Meowth said.

Misty faced Team Rocket. "You're not swiping

anything," she called out. "Pikachu, break the ropes with an electric shock!"

Sparks flew around Pikachu's face. It aimed a charge at the net—but nothing happened!

James laughed. "They're no match for our Pikachu-insulated net."

"It's made from material that absorbs electricity," Jessie added.

I've had it with these clowns, Ash thought. "Let those Pikachu go now!" he demanded.

James detached a small round machine from his belt. "Why don't you check out our website," he taunted. He pushed a button, and a net flew out of the machine, trapping Ash, Misty, and Brock.

"You're not going to get away with this!" Misty cried.

Meowth laughed. "Just watch us!"

Team Rocket disappeared behind the captured Pikachu. Ash saw a large hot-air balloon begin to rise from the clearing. The Pikachu net was tied to the bottom of the balloon basket. Team Rocket was going to lift off—and take all the Pikachu with them!

Ash struggled with the net. "This might be Pika-proof, but it's not people-proof," Ash said. In seconds, the three friends had thrown off their bindings.

Ash ran to the hot-air balloon. The captured Pikachu were high in the air. He couldn't reach them!

"Look—Pikachu has a plan," Misty said.

Pikachu had started chewing on the lines in the net. The wild Pikachu did the same. Soon, they had chewed enough to make a small hole. Pikachu climbed out through the hole and up the net. It hopped into the balloon basket.

"*Meowth!* What's this?" Meowth was startled to see Pikachu.

"Pikachu is distracting Team Rocket," Brock said.

Ash picked up one side of the net that had held them. "Then let's get to work."

Brock and Misty each grabbed a corner of the net.

"Hey, Pikachu! Jump into this! Hurry!" Ash called.

The wild Pikachu heard him. One at a time, they jumped into the net and bounced safely onto the ground.

Back in the balloon basket, Pikachu jumped from Jessie to James to Meowth. Team Rocket couldn't catch the little Pokémon.

"Pikachu! Come down!" Ash called from the ground.

Meowth looked over the edge of the basket at the empty net. "We got a Pika problem down below," he warned.

Jessie and James looked down.

"All our Pikachu are gone," James said.

Jessie eyed Pikachu. "But we do have one left," she said.

Team Rocket charged at Pikachu. Pikachu quickly jumped out of the way. It hopped onto the hot-air balloon and took a bite. Then it leaped to the ground.

"I've got you!" Ash yelled, and caught Pikachu in his arms.

"We're blasting off again!" cried Meowth.

Ash looked up. Pikachu's bite had made a hole in the balloon. Hot air shot from the hole with a powerful blast. The force sent Team Rocket spiraling off into the night sky.

Ash hugged Pikachu. "You did it!"

"Pikachu! Pikachu!"

Pikachu looked up. The wild Pikachu were calling to it.

Pikachu jumped out of Ash's arms and joined the wild Pikachu. *"Pika! Pika!"* They laughed and cheered.

"They're so happy," Misty said. "Isn't it great?"

"Yeah, great," Ash muttered. But deep down, he didn't feel great at all.

CHAPTER 13

Good-Bye, Pikachu

Ash packed up his knapsack. He stepped on the dying embers of the fire until they were all out.

"Ash, you really trained Pikachu well," Brock said.

"Yeah, you did a great job," Misty admitted.

Ash didn't answer. He lifted his knapsack on his shoulder and walked away from the campsite.

Misty ran after him. "Ash, where are you going?"

"I'm leaving," Ash said firmly. "Pikachu is better off without me."

"Pika pi. Pika chu?" Pikachu hopped into the

campsite. It looked at Ash questioningly.

Ash couldn't face Pikachu. He stared at the ground. "Pikachu, you stay here. I know you'll be much happier in the forest with the other Pikachu. They need you."

"Pi?"

"Good-bye, Pikachu," Ash said hoarsely. He ran down the trail without looking behind him.

"Ash, you're crazy!" Misty called out, but Ash didn't answer her. His feet pounded against the dirt as he ran. *If I don't get out of here now,*

I'll never be able to leave Pikachu behind, Ash thought. *It's for the best.*

Images of Pikachu flashed through Ash's mind. Pikachu shocking him in Professor Oak's lab as they met for the very first time. Pikachu leaping in front of him to protect him from the Spearow attack. Pikachu battling the powerful Raichu to defend his honor.

I didn't even ask to choose Pikachu, Ash remembered. *It happened by accident. And*

since then Pikachu's done so much for me! I have to do what's right for Pikachu.

Ash felt a hand grab his shoulder. He stopped, panting. It was Misty. She and Brock had caught up to him.

"Why are you doing this, Ash?" Misty asked.

Ash kicked at the ground. "Pikachu will be better off staying here than traveling around with me," he said.

"But, Ash—"

Ash ignored them and continued on down the trail. The sky was starting to glow with the light of the sunrise.

Behind him, Ash heard Misty and Brock call his name.

Ash spun around.

It was Pikachu!

Pikachu had followed him. It stood against the horizon, in front of the rising sun.

"Pika!" Pikachu called out.

The tiny wild Pikachu scampered up to Pikachu. The other wild Pikachu arrived next. They raised their arms in the air.

"Pikachu! Pikachu!" they cheered.

Pikachu turned and waved to the wild Pikachu. Then it turned around and ran down the trail. Pikachu took a flying leap—right into Ash's arms.

"Pikachu!" Ash hugged the Pokémon.

"I think Pikachu's made its choice," Misty said.

Brock nodded. "That's right, Ash. It looks like Pikachu wants to stay with you."

Ash looked at Pikachu. "I'm sorry, Pikachu. No matter what happens from now on, we'll face it—together."

"Pikachu!" Pikachu replied.

Ash smiled and looked at his Pikachu, Misty, and Brock as the sun rose over the forest. Ash knew that as long as he had his friends, he was ready for a new day.

And a new adventure!

Build your

Pokémon™

library!

Trainers, are you ready?

Get creative and put your skills to the test!

Flip over this book for another awesome Pokémon story!